ENDANGERED

KICKSTART
LOS ANGELES · CALIFORNIA

ENDANGERED

WRITTEN BY
JOSH WILLIAMSON

ART & COVER BY
JUAN SANTACRUZ

COLORS BY
JUANMANUAL TUMBURUS

LETTERS & DESIGN BY BILL TORTOLINI

EDITED BY JIMMY PALMIOTTI

PRODUCED BY KICKSTART COMICS INC.

For Kickstart Comics Inc:
Samantha Shear, Managing Editor

ENDANGERED. FEBURARY 2011. FIRST PRINTING. Published by Kickstart Comics Inc (480 Washington Ave North, Suite 201, Ketchum, ID. 83340). ©2011 Kickstart Comics, Inc. ENDANGERED. "ENDANGERED," the Titles logos, and the likeness of all featured characters are trademarks of Kickstart Comics, Inc. All rights reserved. Any resemblance to actual persons (living or dead), events, institutions, or locales, without satiric intent, is coincidental. No portion of this publication may be reproduced or transmitted, in any form or by any means, without the express written permission of Kickstart Comics, Inc.
PRINTED IN USA.

Address correspondence to: Kickstart Comics Inc.
480 Washington Ave., North Suite 201, Ketchum, ID. 83340

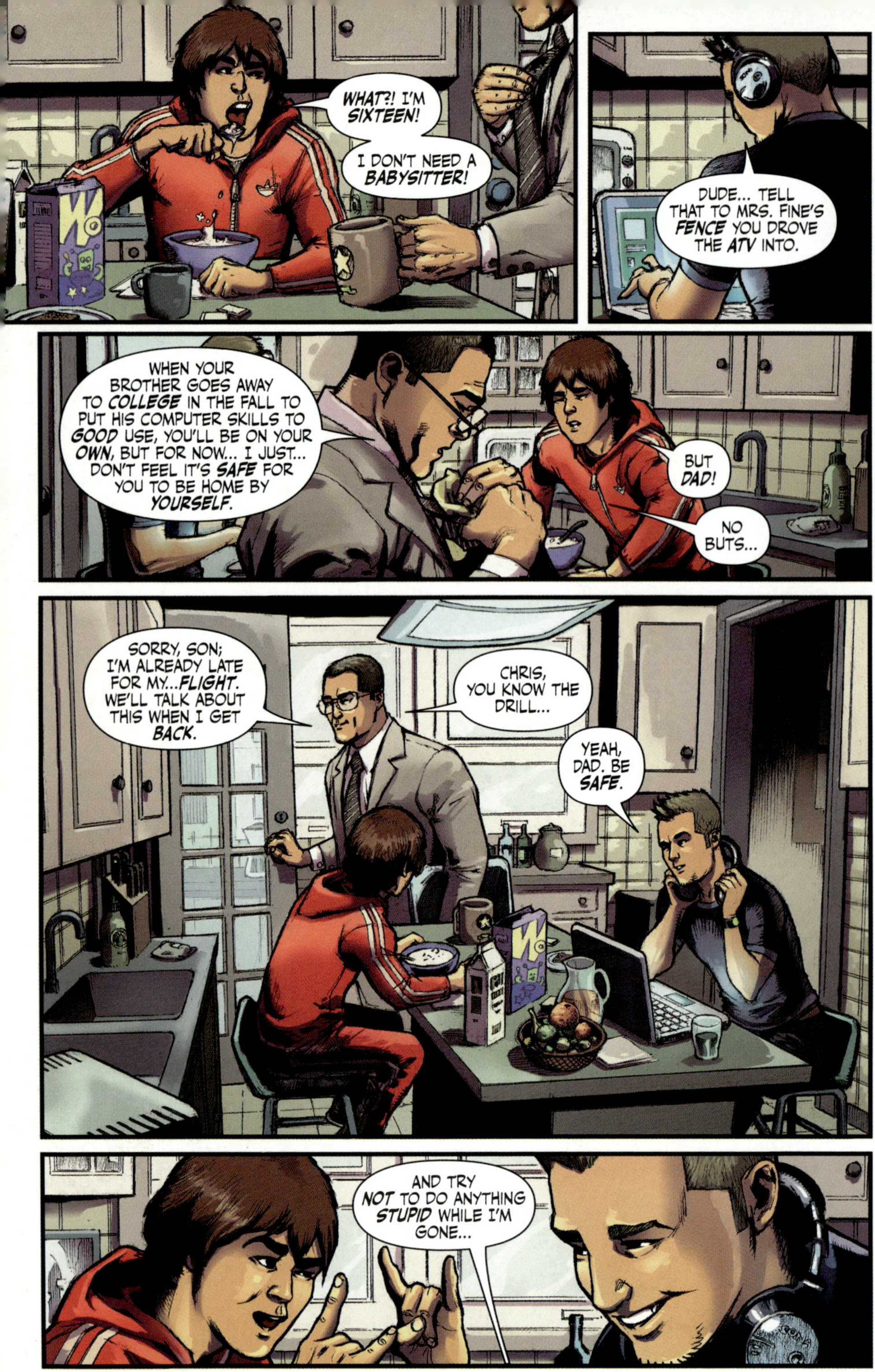

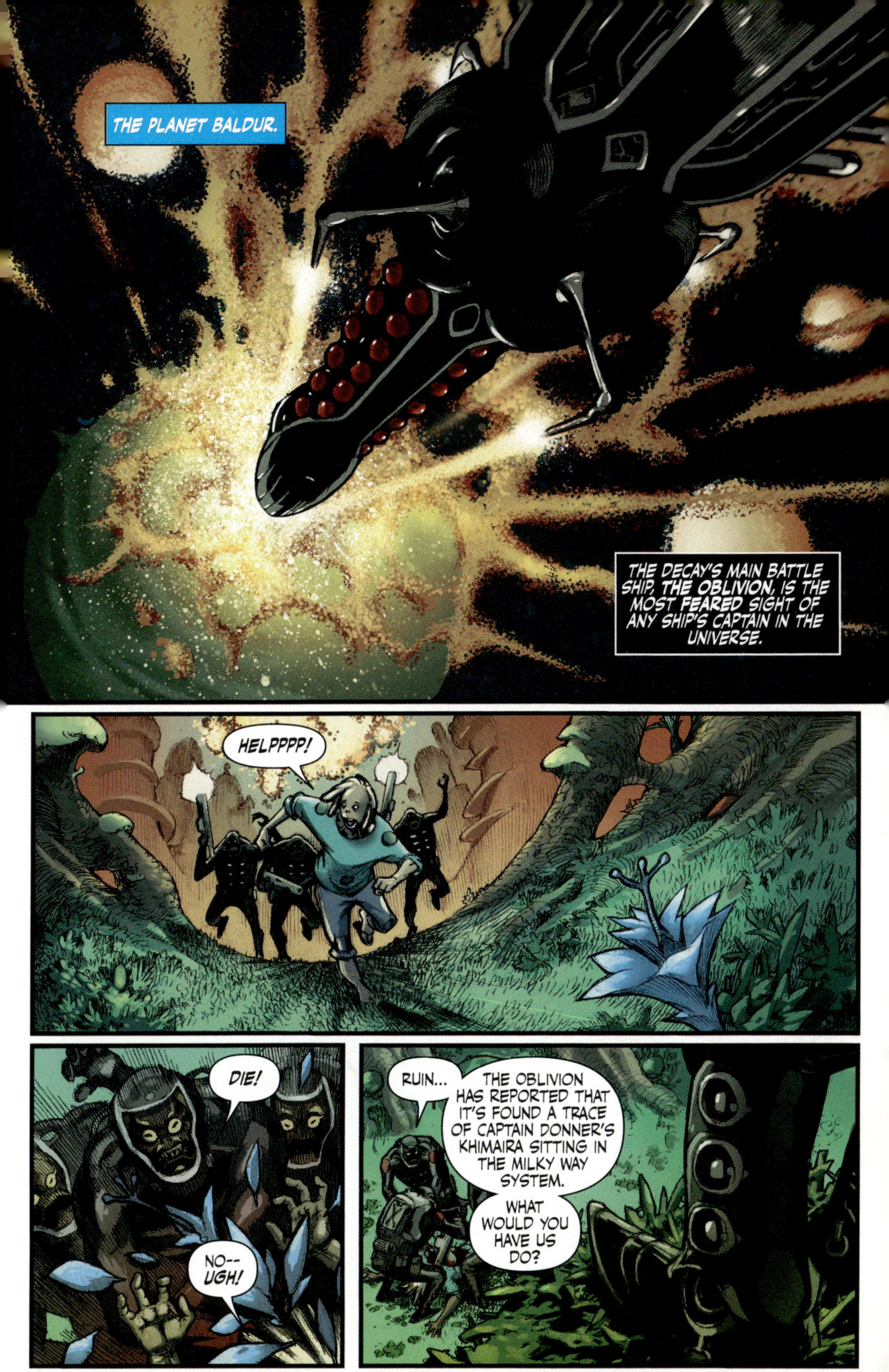

RUN...

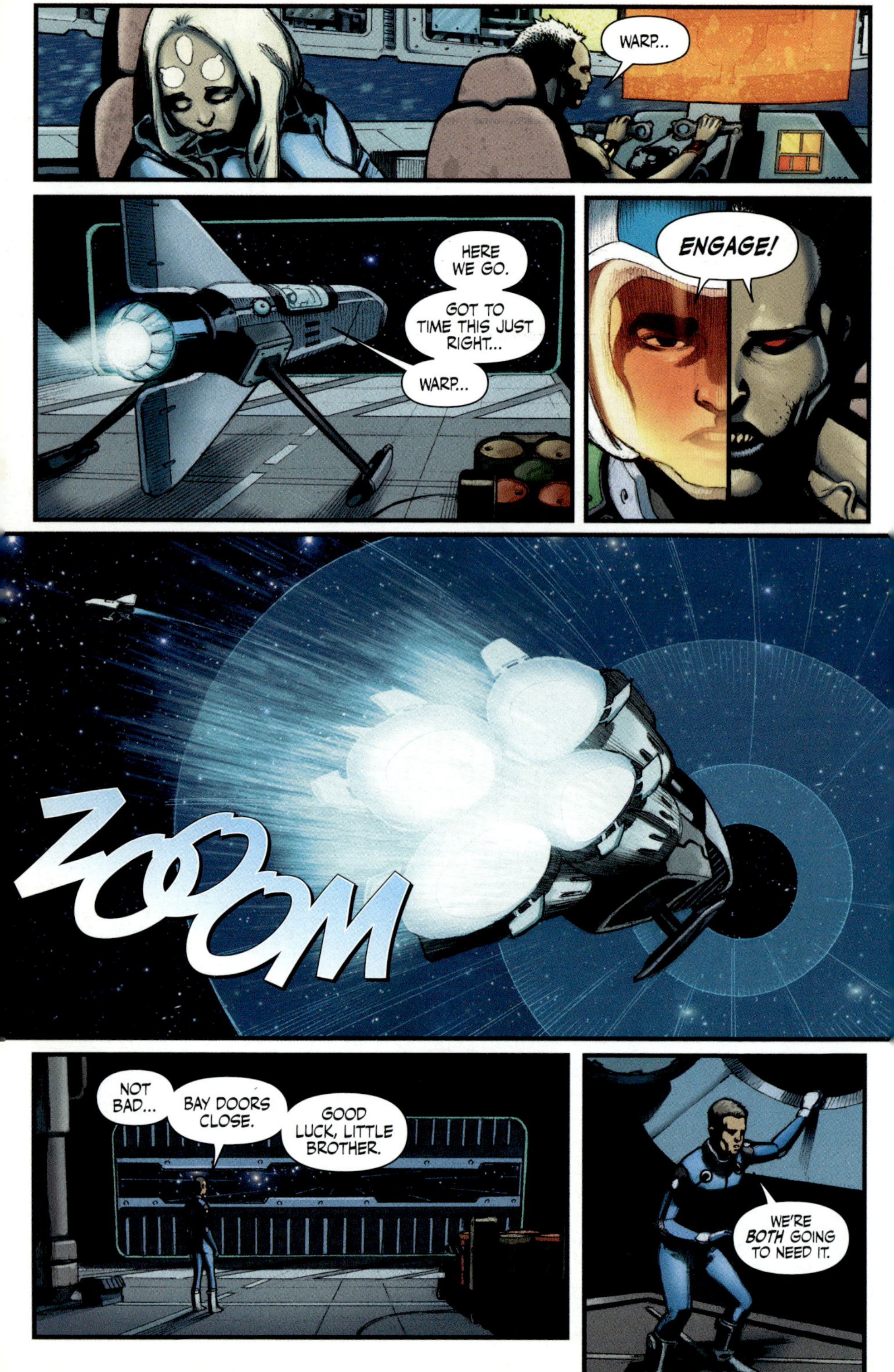

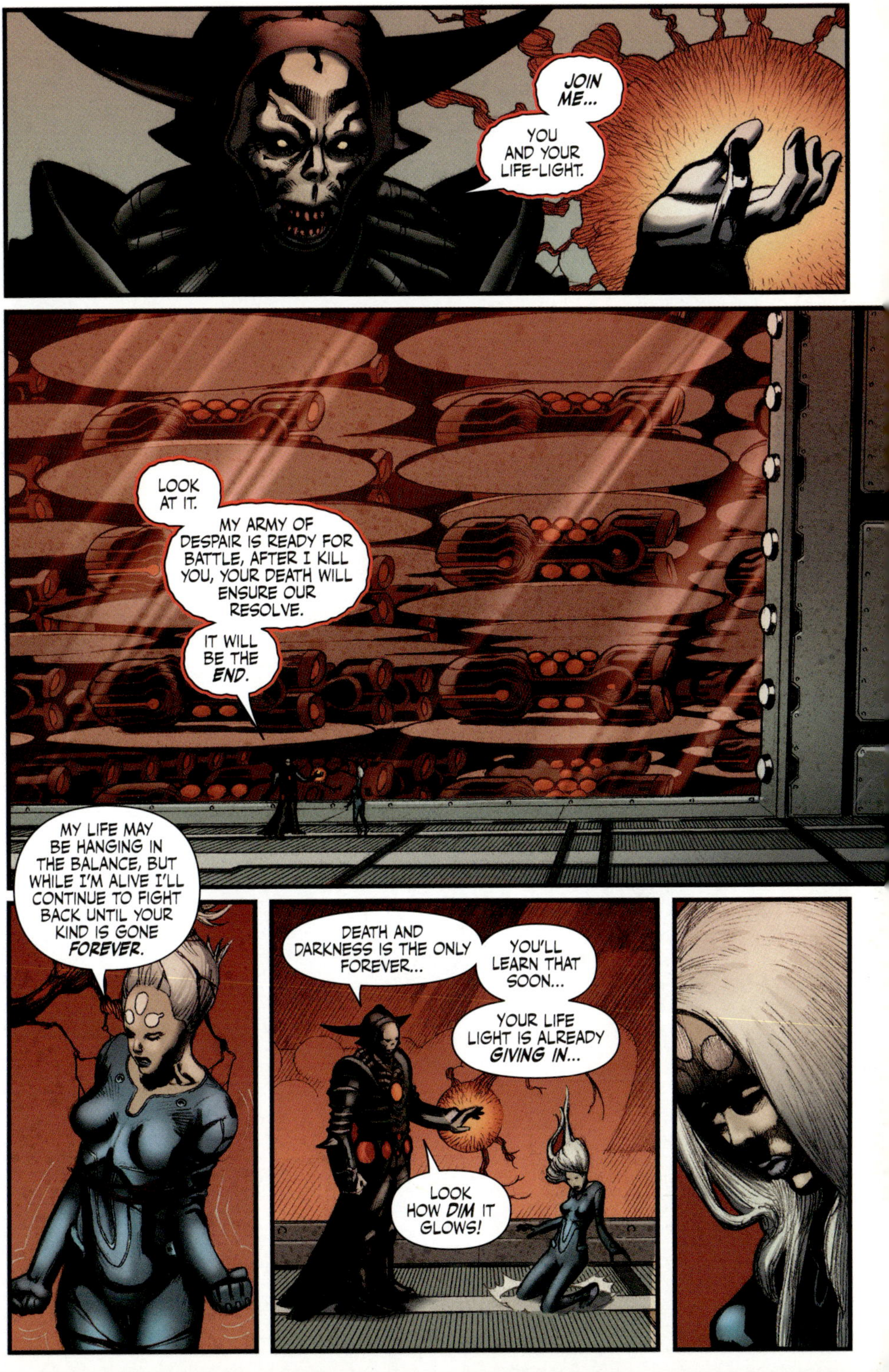

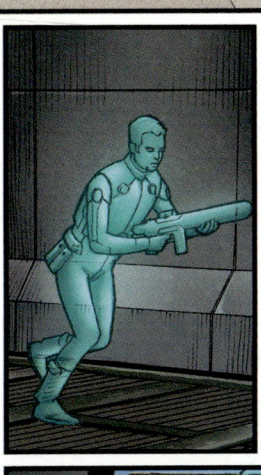

I'M DISAPPOINTED...

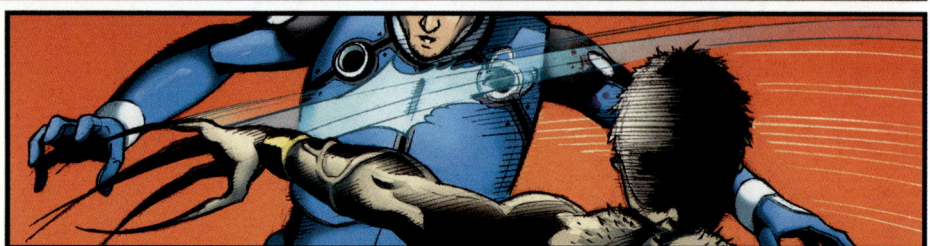

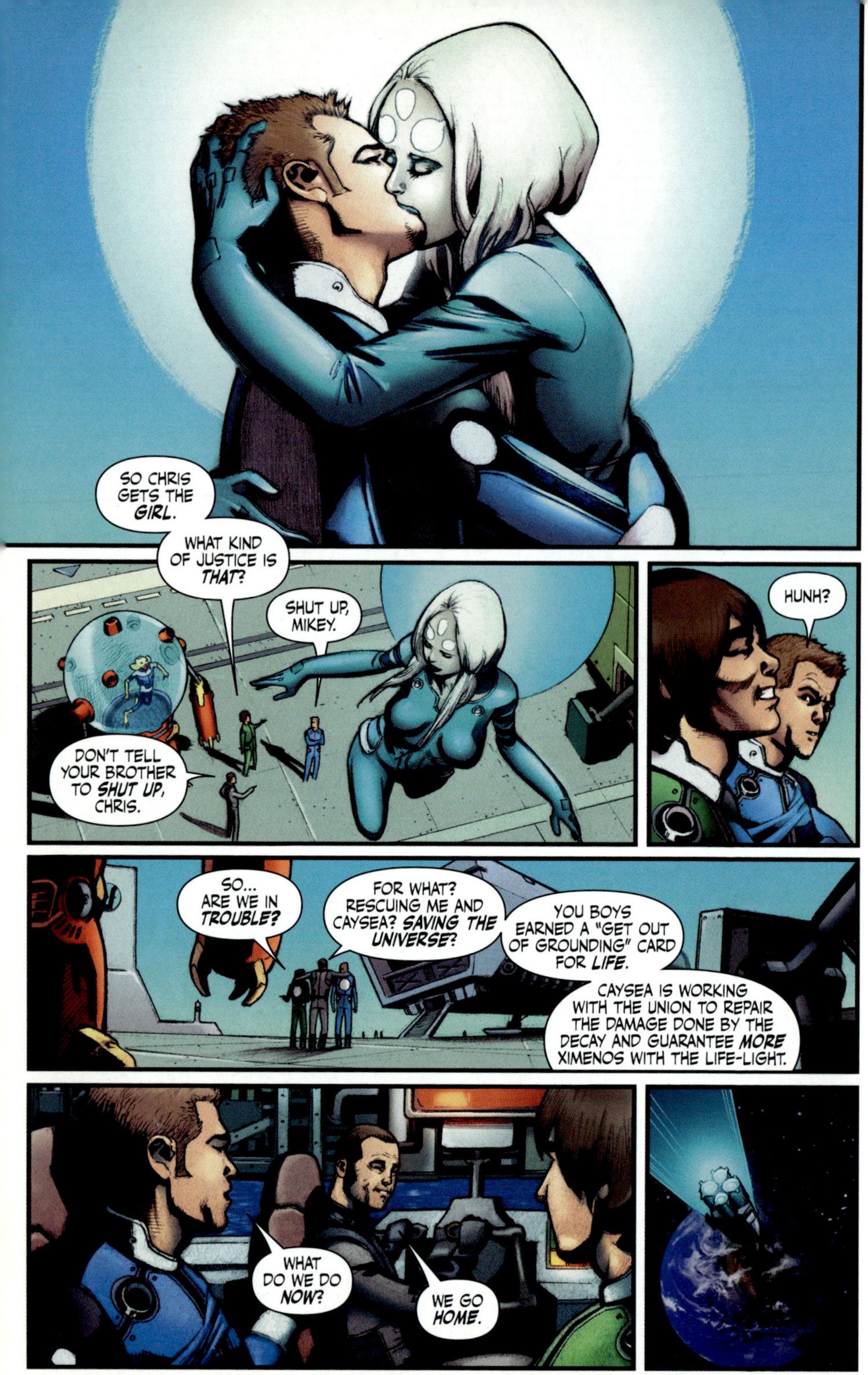

THE END

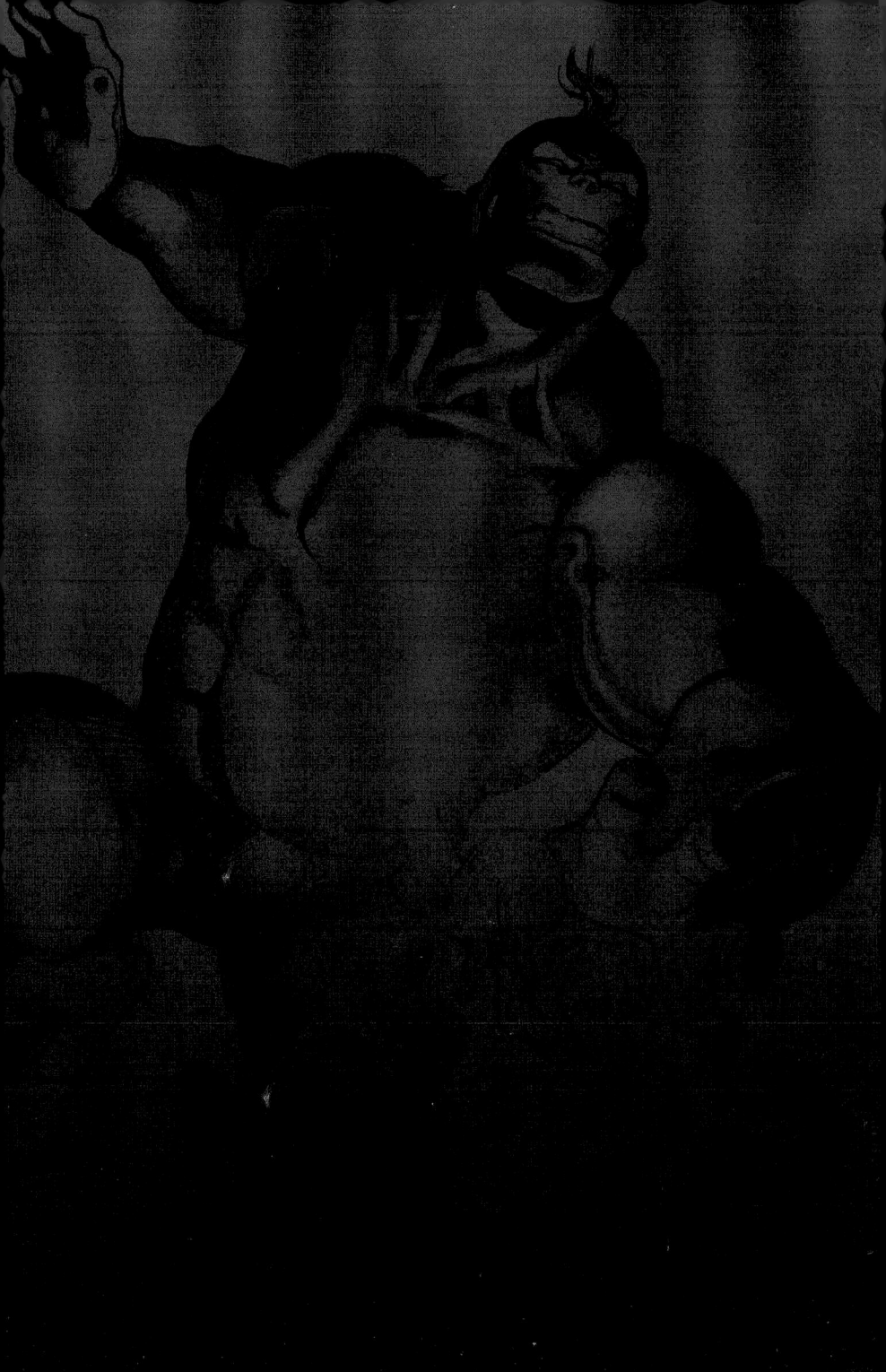

Divine Wind
WRITTEN BY JEFF Y. AMANO

HAKATA BAY, JAPAN

"The other day, a boy cut off the head of a snake. His parents cried out to me, wanting to know if their son committed a karmic transgression."

"I told them to reward their son with a sweet bean cake."

"Had the snake entered my temple, it would be well-cared for. Had the snake remained in the forest, he would enjoy the bounty of the wild. But it ventured into the boy's home and paid the price of trespass."

"That is the Way of things."

COMING SOON FROM

NOVEMBER 20, 1274

"The gods took care of the rest."

"But Kublai Khan is sure to return."

KNOWBODYS

WRITTEN BY MATT MAIELLARO

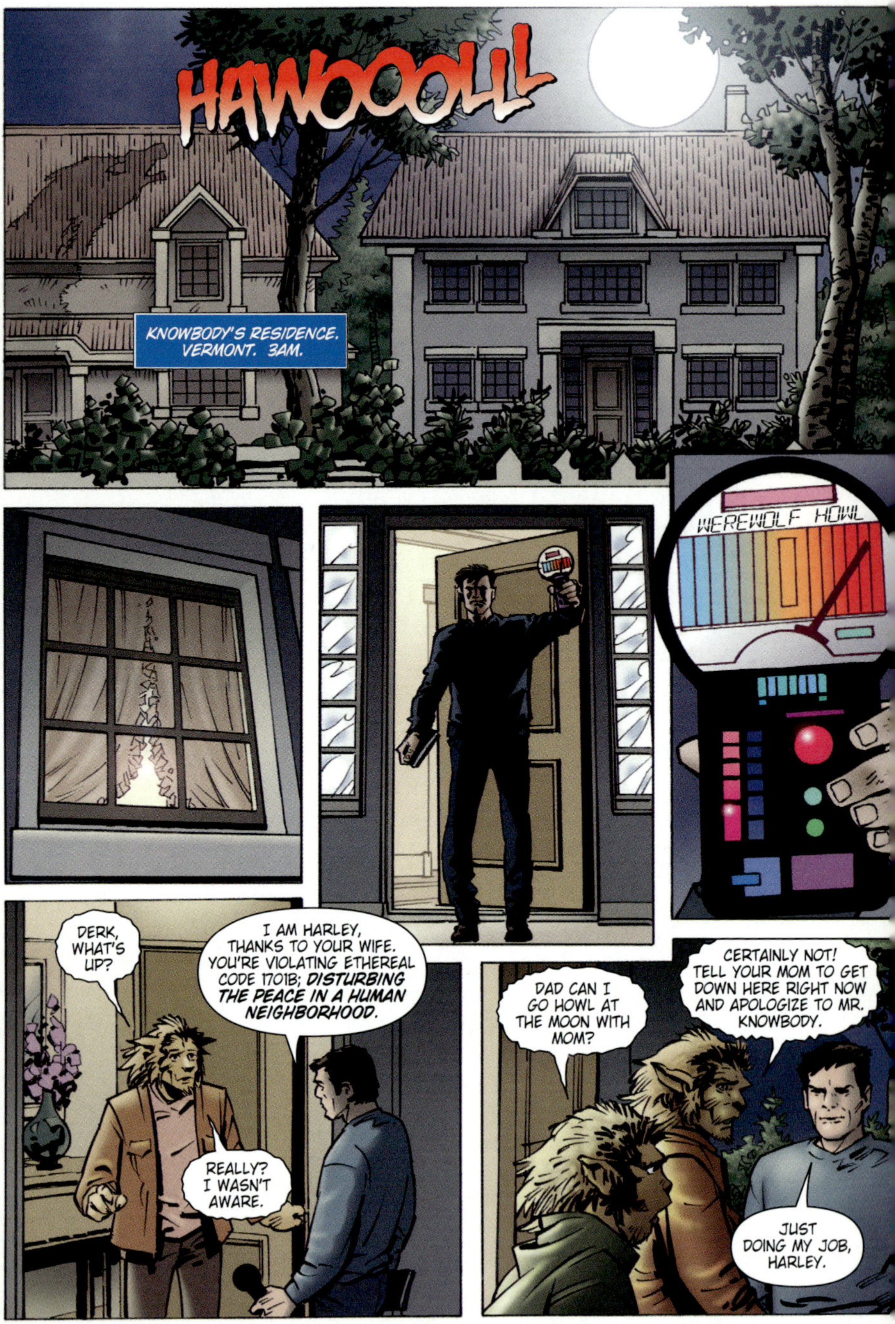

COMING SOON FROM **KICKSTART**

COMING SOON FROM **KICKSTART**

Check out these great comics

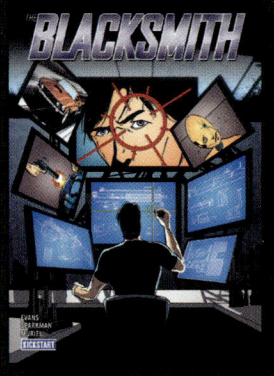
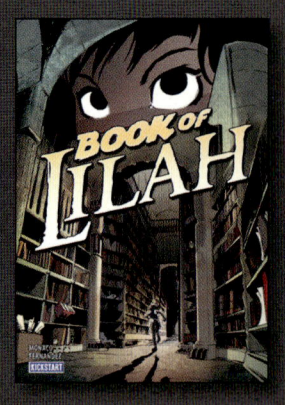
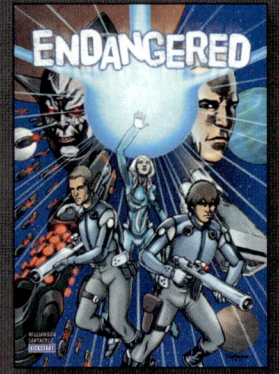
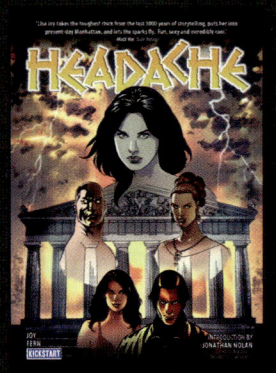
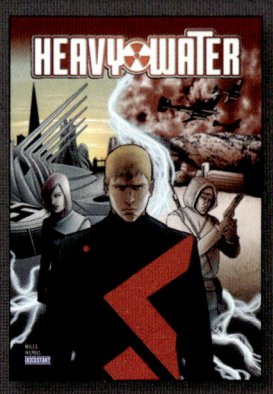

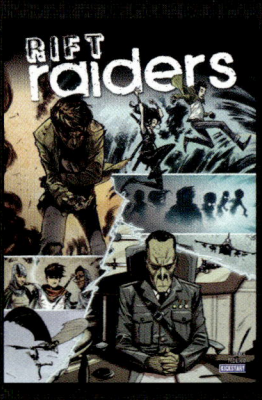
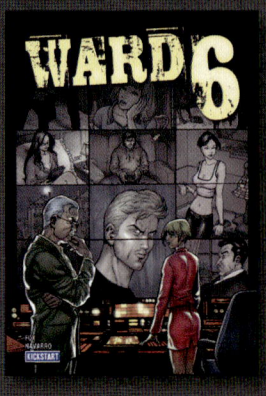

www.KICKSTARTCOMICS.com
FOLLOW US ON FACEBOOK AND TWITTER @KICKSTARTCOMICS